SCARY SHORT STORIES FOR TEENS
BOOK 2

A COLLECTION OF BONE
CHILLING, CREEPY, HORROR
SHORT STORIES

BRYCE NEALHAM

CONTENTS

STORY 1

KNOCKING AT MY DOOR

I had a single dorm my first semester of sophomore year. It was in the corner of the floor, kind of secluded from the rest of the dorm rooms.

Since it was in its own little section, you had to turn a corner to even see the door. It was nice because I'd be able to still talk with friends on my floor, invite people over to my room and still have privacy when it was time to do homework or go to sleep.

A few weeks into the semester while studying for a bio exam the silence was interrupted by a noise. It took me a bit to realize it was a light tapping on my door. It was so light that I almost didn't even hear it.

I yelled "come in" but the door didn't open so I got up to open it; nobody was there. I walked around the corner to look down the hall but found nobody.

Someone was obviously messing with me. I went back to my bed and continued studying this time leaving the door open. Nobody came back.

The next night, a few minutes after shutting the lamp in my bedroom to go to bed, the tapping on the door returned only this time it was much louder; more of a knocking sound.

I called out "who is it" and again the knocking stopped and nobody answered. I got out of my bed quickly and opened the door to see my small private corridor was void of any people again.

I ran the ten feet from my door to the corner to look down the main hallway of the floor and saw nobody.

The next morning I asked some of the other kids in the dorm if they had been messing with me but everyone said no.

That night I woke up after having been asleep for three hours; someone was knocking on my door again this time louder than ever. I had trouble deciding whether to open the door or not this time.

With a bout of courage I hopped up and opened the door but as usual, nobody was there. This time I full-on sprinted down the tiny corridor isolating my room and when I turned the corner I saw the back of somebody disappearing behind the far corner on the opposite side of the hallway.

I ran as fast as I could down the hallway and as I turned to the next hallway I saw a door at the end of the hallway close with a bang. It wasn't a dorm room, it was the dorm bathroom.

I felt like I was ready to confront whoever this joker was so I pushed open the bathroom door with force. The light was off so I turned it on expecting to see somebody hiding in there, but I didn't see anyone.

My first instinct was to check the two bathroom stalls which were both shut. I got on my hands and knees and looked under the two stalls. Two heavy black boots could be seen from underneath one of the stall doors.

I took a deep breath and pushed the stall open. I was suddenly confused. There were the boots sitting on the floor but no person to wear them.

At that moment I heard a creepy giggling sound from inside the room. It wasn't a feminine or childlike one, it was a kind of laughing that I could only imagine to be that of a really old crazy man.

All of a sudden, my confidence disappeared and was replaced with fear. I ran back to my room and shut the door. I hopped back in my bed and started texting every friend I had. Of course everybody was asleep though so I received no replies that night.

The knocking happened one more time that night. I ignored it. It continued for about 30 seconds before whoever or whatever was out there finally gave up.

I spoke to everybody on my floor the next day. Nobody else heard any knocking and everybody swore they weren't pranking me. Everybody seemed sincere.

I don't know why this person chose to harass me or who this person was. I don't even know if it even was a person.

STORY 2

WHO GOES THERE?

For the past three years or so I've worked as an overnight security guard at a mall. It used to be that the mall didn't require an overnight person but vandalism started to become a problem.

Most of the time, I would drive around the parking lot all night listening to my car radio. Now and then I'd kick some skateboarders out of the parking lot or investigate a suspicious person lurking about. Other than that, I'd say the job was pretty tame.

Maybe three months in, I experienced something a little bit stranger. I noticed that the light to one of the shops was on while driving around the parking lot. This was surprising to me considering no one had snuck past me as of yet, so of course I parked the car and headed inside the mall to catch the potential thieves.

As I approached the shop I didn't hear the sound of anyone rummaging through the inventory and sure enough the shop was empty. As a matter of fact even the security gate was still down.

Only the shop owners had access to the security gates so I couldn't really do anything about the light being on. I decided to head back out to my car and chill out for a bit.

An hour went by with no incident but as I was circling around the entrance to the mall I saw another light was on inside.

It was the same scene repeated; the shop light was on but the security gate was still closed. I even tugged on the damn thing to see if someone heard me coming.

Nope. Everything was locked and secure. Suddenly, I heard a click from behind me. A previous light that was on now had turned off. Was my mind playing tricks on me?

I swear I saw someone run behind the counter and hide. I think about now is a good time to mention I was running on three hours of sleep for the past 48 hours. I was tired and blaming these occurrences just simply on the lack of sleep.

I shined my flashlight into the shop and scanned the area. I didn't find anything. Then, behind me there was another click sound.

I know I saw someone standing in there this time so I simply called out, "You can either leave with me or you can leave with the police".

They didn't move. Whoever it was, just stood next to the light switch, totally still. I approached the gate and turned my light in the direction of the light switch but there was no one standing there.

I did see that a clothes rack was fairly close to the switch so maybe the light was catching the clothes just right and was casting a shadow. That was the most logical explanation I could think of at least.

I was pretty spooked from the events of that night but after a few weeks I had forgotten about the whole thing.

My patrols were nothing special for a while after that. I think my next incident happened around my one-year anniversary as a guard.

It was winter and I was inside the mall heading to one of the bathrooms to relieve myself. I walked in and the lights turned on automatically. I walked towards the urinals when suddenly one of the toilets flushed.

I jumped a little more than I would like to admit. It scared the crap out of me. The mall was closed; there shouldn't be anyone in the bathroom at this time.

The toilets in the mall were motion activated much like every other mall in the world. I checked all the stalls and they were all empty.

I'll spare you the details, but after checking the stalls I took a seat in one of them. I had a YouTube video playing on my phone.

While I was sitting doing my thing, I heard a tapping sound coming from the stall next to me. I glanced down to my left and saw a pair of large black boots with the toes pointing towards my stall.

A shot of pure fear ran through me as I brought my eyes up above the stall and sure enough there was the tallest man I'd ever seen standing over the stall staring down at me.

The strangest thing is that even though the lights were on in the bathroom this person was in total shadow; I couldn't see a face. All I saw was a dark shape.

Also, whoever or whatever this was, they must have been over seven feet tall because their head was almost touching the ceiling.

When he saw me notice him, he ducked back over to his side of the stall. I hopped off the toilet, pulled my pants back up and ran out. I stopped in front of the neighboring stall and kicked in the door.

The damn thing was empty; except for a large pair of black boots sitting in the same spot I had seen them.

My heart was thumping like crazy. I went back to my car as quickly as possible after that. If I remember correctly, this happened at around 4:00 in the morning. Once again, I accredited all this to my lack of sleep…but up to this day I can't be sure of that.

STORY 3

HOUSE FROM HELL

I lived in a house from hell for a couple of weeks. I was a college student and my parents were paying for a house for me to live in. Yeh, I know, I am spoilt.

Anyway, the house was modest, nothing fancy or huge and I was happy with it…well for the first few days anyway.

Things quickly started getting strange one rainy Saturday. I was watching TV for a few hours when I heard a scrape on my living room floor. I looked around the room thinking an animal got into the house or something. I saw nothing and sat back down to resume watching TV.

The rain continued throughout the rest of the day and into the night which made for an excuse to not go out. I stayed in watching more TV in the living room. I perked up when I heard something from the kitchen.

I walked over to the kitchen doorway and there in the middle of the dark kitchen was a box of Cheerios on the floor. Hundreds of the tiny O's were scattered all over the place.

I had no idea how that could have happened; nevertheless I dropped to my knees and began cleaning up the Cheerios off the floor.

As I was doing so I heard the old wooden floor creak as if someone was slowly walking over them. It was by the kitchen table. I looked up but of course nobody was there.

I knew I was going crazy now because every little sound must have been making me paranoid. I cleaned the Cheerios and went back to watching TV.

The thunder outside was getting louder as the bulk of the storm seemed to be passing overhead, yet I found it to be strangely relaxing. That was the last thing I remember, appreciating the sound of the storm outside, before waking up from what seemed to be an hour-long doze.

The TV was still on but that wasn't what woke me. I actually woke up to a bang or a thud from downstairs. I turned off the TV and marched straight to bed.

The next day was normal as was the day after that. It wasn't until the next gray rainy day that strange things started happening again.

I woke up in my bed that morning feeling like I had been drinking for hours the night before. I felt sicker than I'd ever felt with any hangover and the strange thing is that I hadn't even been drinking.

I didn't do much walking around that day, the gloomy dark weather only made me more bedridden. I left the TV in my bedroom on all day just as background noise with a garbage pail by my side in case I had to puke.

At midday I muted the TV after hearing sounds coming from above me; the attic. The attic door was actually in my bedroom and most of the attic was built over that bedroom. It wasn't just once though, I heard it three or four more times.

I managed to get out of bed despite the fact that every time I moved I wanted to puke. I reached up and pulled the attic door down. I then picked up an old baseball bat and climbed up the steps.

I pulled the light switch cord down to light up the attic. There were a few old boxes that must have belonged to the previous owner scattered about but I couldn't see any living things.

I climbed back down quickly because I was kind of scared of that attic. There were no more noises until late that night. I woke up to the familiar sound of a thud from up in the attic again. It gave me chills.

I decided to take another look. I pulled the string to the attic door back down, took my baseball bat once again and climbed up the stairs.

I made myself angry and screamed in the most intimidating voice I could but before I could turn the light on I heard the sound of a child giggling in the pitch-black corner.

Words cannot describe the feeling of weightlessness, the feeling of my insides dropping inside of my body, the fear that I felt at that moment.

I didn't stick around this time. I was feeling sick and weak but was able to muster enough energy to get the hell out of that house fast.

I was so scared that I don't even remember running. I called my dad in the cold rain and asked him to pick me up.

I explained everything the best I could. My parents saw how emotional I was about this and in a weird sense I think they believed me.

I packed all of my things up with my parents the next day and moved back home. To this day I'm convinced what I experienced in that house was something paranormal.

STORY 4

BUMP IN THE NIGHT

I am 22 years old living with my brother, Andrew in a house we share. I have never had anything severely strange or abnormal happen to me in my life but there was this one week that I experienced this strange series of events.

It started on what I thought would be a normal night like any other. I was in the kitchen washing the dishes before getting ready for bed. Suddenly a plastic cup came crashing to the floor.

The sound of it made me jump and spin around from the sink. I saw the blue plastic cup bounce a few times then fall dead on the floor. This was one of the cups that sit on the top shelf of the cabinet.

I knew it had to have been sitting upright though I had no idea what kind of force could have knocked it off the cabinet. It made no logical sense.

I picked it up and put it back on the cabinet. That wasn't the last strange event that night though. While in bed with the blinds shut there was suddenly a strange very faint glow in my room. It came through the blinds.

I flipped over onto my side and tried to peek under the crack at the bottom of the blinds but I couldn't see anything. Honestly, as weird as it sounds, I was so comfortable in bed I just dismissed the bright beam as something like a street light turning on or something. I had no reason to suspect anything paranormal.

The next day I was home alone while Andrew was at work. It was dark and stormy and the house was constantly rumbling from the thunder outside. So, when I heard a cup fall from the kitchen I associated it with the thunder.

I went to the kitchen to pick it up and realized it was the same blue plastic cup I'd carefully put back on the cabinet yesterday.

There was no way thunder could have knocked it down from there. I put it on the counter and stood there confused and a bit shaken.

While looking around the kitchen not knowing what to think I then heard a creak in the floor above me. The room above me was actually my bedroom.

I went to the stairs and called up for Andrew but I instantly remembered he wasn't home. Maybe it was the thunder shaking the whole house, but still I had to check my room just for peace of mind.

I went up the stairs to my room and turned on the lights. My room is square shaped with two big closets; nothing special. I looked around and the room was clear as where the closets.

I shut the light and went back downstairs. That night when Andrew got home I had a discussion with him about the strange events that had been taking place. He said he hadn't been aware of any of it. For the rest of the night things were normal and I fell asleep with ease.

A few hours later I suddenly jerked out of sleep; wide awake. It was still dark. I checked my phone; it was 2:00 in the morning.

Just as I rolled back on my side and shut my eyes I heard the distinct sound of a finger tapping on my window. I could feel my heart in my throat. I didn't know why someone would be tapping on my window but I didn't want to see who it could be out there.

After a few seconds of thought I realized that my window was on the second floor of the house, therefore nobody could be on the outside of my window…unless they were on a ladder.

I pushed the sheets off my body and flipped to face the window. There was no one there. I lifted the blind and there was no one outside either.

I knew that I had heard something. I knew I hadn't been imagining or dreaming it. I ran to my brother's room and started freaking out.

I don't know whether he believed me or not. Quite frankly I don't think I'd believe me if I hadn't experienced it. I slept in the living room that night.

It's been three weeks now without any paranormal incidents I never believed in the supernatural until this happened.

STORY 5

THE RED BALL

I own a small house on a big property in the rural part of New York and I go up there a bunch of times a year in the winter months to go skiing.

There's a neighbor up there that I have never spoken to and there's a fence that separates our two yards. On the other side of my house are woods for miles.

There's another neighbor further down the road across the street and I'd met him a number of times because he happens to go skiing too. So we got to know each other based off that.

I went up to the house this past January for the first time in the season. As I walked up to the front door I heard a kid laughing nearby in the neighbor's houses direction; I figured they had kids, which was news to me.

Stepping into the house for the first time each season was always weird because it would be empty for a majority of the year. I'd have to turn on the water, heat and everything, hoping that it would all still be working well.

On the first night I slept like a baby after the four-hour drive from Connecticut which helped me to recharge. The next morning after eating breakfast and changing into my ski gear I went outside and found a big red ball sitting in the snow on my front lawn.

It wasn't there the day before so I assumed it belonged to the neighbors. I took the ball and threw it over the fence separating our properties. I then went off to the ski lodge to meet my friends and we spent the day skiing.

When I got back, it was already dark out. I had eaten dinner with my friends so I was ready to go to bed.

Walking to the front door I noticed that once again that big red ball was sitting on my front lawn. This was beginning to feel a bit odd but once again I threw that red ball over the fence not wanting to think about it too much.

I woke up in the middle of that night to laughter outside. It was a kid's laughter. I looked at my bedside clock and it read 3:00 a.m. A kid playing outside at this hour…that made no sense so I went to look out my window.

I couldn't see any kids though and now the laughter had stopped, however I did see something sitting on my front lawn. I couldn't tell from the window so I went outside into the snow with my slippers and robe and saw that red ball once again sitting in the snow.

I got chills as I saw it in the same spot once again. I took the ball and this time instead of throwing it over the fence I brought it inside my house and went back to sleep.

The next morning before going skiing again I walked over to the neighbor's house, knocked on the door and finally introduced myself. Surprisingly he was an elderly man who seemed completely innocent.

I questioned him about the child's laughter I kept hearing and the ball that kept ending up on my lawn. He told me there were no kids living in the neighborhood.

I got those chills again. I thanked him, shook his hand and went back to my house. I left the red ball in my living room and drove back up the mountain and had another day of skiing with my friends.

When I got back to the house that night I was completely exhausted and ready to go home the next day. I threw all my stuff on the couch and figured I'd pack it all up tomorrow. I literally crashed onto the bed as my whole body was sore and I fell straight to sleep.

An hour or so later, I woke up to a kids laughter outside again. I jumped out of bed and ran to the window to look outside. Once again, there was the red ball sitting in the snow.

I ran to the living room and tore the room upside down looking for the ball I had left inside. I still know to this day I'd left it in there; I remember seeing it just before going to bed. It wasn't anywhere in the house now.

I suddenly didn't feel alone in the house. I turned on every light as I packed up all my wet gear into my bag. I threw everything in the bag so I'd be ready to go if I needed to get out fast.

I couldn't figure it out. Did someone break into my home while I slept just so they could take the red ball? That didn't make any sense, especially seeing as the night before

I made sure all the doors and windows were locked. I looked around and there were no signs of any break-in.

I left the lights on and went back to my room shutting off only those lights. I looked out the window and far behind the red ball standing in the snow was what looked like a kid.

This was a kid just standing stiff, looking towards my window. I ducked down and closed the blinds. I closed the blinds to every window in my house.

I tried my best to just go to sleep and ignore it, passing it off as a hallucination from being too tired. It was a long hour before my exhaustion overcame my fear and I fell asleep.

I woke up the next morning, skipped breakfast, packed up the car and began to drive out of my parked spot. I turned one last time to look at the house and to my shock there was the red ball again. It sat on the same spot on my front lawn.

The shocking part was that while I was packing my car there was no ball there.

To this day I can't figure out how whoever was out there got into my house to take the ball out in the first place. I also couldn't figure out that creepy child's laughter. It still haunts.

I never went back to the house. I sold it off. God help the new owners.

STORY 6

SLENDERMAN HOTEL

I never believed in the supernatural until this happened. I once took a road trip from New Hampshire to Florida. I had to stop at a hotel to sleep overnight. It was some old somewhat dilapidated hotel that rested off the highway on a quiet road.

There were two cars in the parking lot so there were definitely not a lot of guests staying. The lady at the front desk was very robotic and seemed bored with her job. She seemed to fit the atmosphere of the hotel perfectly.

The lobby was full of tacky chairs and tables you'd expect to find put out on the curb. The wallpaper was dated and equally tacky. It didn't matter though; I wasn't staying there for the luxury. It was just a room for the night and for the convenience.

It was late when I checked in so when I got in the room all I did was take out my toothbrush and brush my teeth before jumping into the hotel bed. I turned out the lamp next to the bed and tried to go to sleep not looking forward to the long day of driving I had ahead of me the next day.

Suddenly there was a knock at the door. I looked at the bedside clock, it was almost midnight. I went to the door and looked through the peephole. Apparently the peephole didn't work though because I couldn't see out into the hallway: all I saw was black.

I looked down at the crack under the door but didn't see any outlines of feet blocking the light so I opened the door just a little bit to peek into the hallway.

I didn't see anyone standing in front of the door. I opened it fully and then peeked down both sides of the hallway; it was clear.

I suddenly questioned if someone in this relatively vacant hotel was pranking me. I shut the door, locked it with the bolt this time and went to lie back down in the bed.

Then it happened again, a knock at the door. This time I jumped out of the bed ran to the door and checked the peephole again. Shockingly all I saw was the empty hallway outside, but this time I could actually see through the peephole.

I unbolted the door and opened it. I looked down both sides of the hallway and again there was no one around. This was where I drew the line. I grabbed the key to the room and went to the lady at the front desk.

I told her someone kept knocking on my door and politely asked her to check the cameras to see who it could be. She said they didn't have cameras in the hallways. Her reaction also wasn't what I was hoping for, she was very nonchalant.

In a calm voice she told me that there was only one other guest in the whole building that night. Then she just stared blankly at me.

I'm not sure how she thought her response properly acknowledged my concern or what she expected me to say but I could tell she wouldn't be of any help so I left her and went back to my room. I locked the door with the bolt again making sure it was locked.

I decided to put on my headphones and listen to one of those eight hour sleep relaxation audios. This would not only help me get to sleep but block out any possible future sounds from whoever was deciding to mess with me.

I was having trouble sleeping. I flipped from my side to my back just looking around the room. My head froze with me staring at one dark spot in the corner of the room.

I sat up to try to get a closer look at what I thought I was seeing. I didn't believe what I was looking at. I swear, there was a giant humanoid figure around 8 foot just standing there in the corner...facing me.

It was very thin with long lanky arms and long pointy fingers. Its head was almost touching the ceiling. I felt a sudden rush of horror in my body that compelled me to jump across the bed and flick on the lamp.

When the room lit up there was nothing in that corner. I simply sat there with my heart beating very fast. I gave myself a couple of minutes to calm down before shutting the light back off and laying back down on my side.

I still had the headphones in my ears playing the relaxation audio; it helped calm me down a little bit but that wouldn't last.

I sat back up and examined the room again. In the darkness I looked towards the corner where I had seen the strange figure. Again, in the corner I saw that humanoid shape once more. I crawled to the edge of the bed to get a closer look. I wasn't dreaming.

I watched in fear as this slender man began to move its long arms upwards. At that moment I dove to turn on the lamp. As I turned to look at the corner I discovered that there was nothing there once again.

I didn't stick around this time. I packed up my things in a matter of seconds and left the room. I gave the key to the woman at the counter and told her I was checking out early.

She stared at me blankly, not saying a word. I stormed out the front door of the hotel, jumped in my car and drove out of there.

I continued driving until I found another hotel where I stayed the night. I didn't get a wink of sleep.

STORY 7

ODD EVELYN

I used to work as a maid for some old lady for a couple of weeks when I was 20. She had a really big and old house on a property that could have been beautiful had she actually taken care of it.

She had two acres of land surrounded by woods in three directions. The interior was really dark and mostly made from wood.

She would often keep the curtains shut in all the rooms for some reason. I would sometimes open the curtains to let some sunlight in only to find that she'd close them again.

She lit some rooms by candle which made the house seem even more prehistoric for me and to top it off the wood floors were so creaky.

The old woman's name was Evelyn and she was around 80 years old. The kind of work she would have me do would be mostly physical stuff that she couldn't do very well anymore. Things like sweeping, dusting, cleaning dishes, doing laundry, sorting mail and other things of that sort.

One weekend Evelyn asked me to sleep there for a night or two because she had some extra work for me. The house had four bedrooms yet she lived alone so staying over wasn't an issue for me. It meant I could earn more.

This takes place over the course of a Friday and technically a Saturday as well. I arrived as per usual on Friday. I dropped my backpack full of my clothes and cosmetics onto the bed and as I turned to the door. I saw Evelyn standing by the doorway. She had a creepy way about her and this entrance was no exception.

She didn't say hello which wasn't as weird as it sounds but she did instruct me to clean the bedroom right away. After that she just told me to simply straighten up the whole house and then she went upstairs.

I didn't see her for the rest of the day but I would occasionally hear her walking around upstairs in her bedroom. It was weird because she would seem to walk back and forth as though she was pacing. There were no TVs in this house so I didn't know what she could have been doing.

One thing that I found bizarre was how protective she was of her basement; she made it clear it was completely off-limits and she didn't want me going down there.

Nighttime came and I went to bed early. This was before smartphones were a thing so I didn't even know what time it was; it was probably nine or ten o'clock.

For the first few hours everything was peaceful, however I still had trouble falling asleep given that it was the most uncomfortable bed I'd ever slept in.

It felt like hours later that I started hearing footsteps outside my room on the creaky floors. It sounded like Evelyn was passing my room really slowly. Maybe she was just going to the bathroom.

A few minutes later I heard her footsteps again but then she stopped right outside my door. I sat up and listened. I could hear the creaking from behind the door of Evelyn standing there and it was starting to creep me out.

After a few minutes she finally walked away. I heard her go down the stairs and then I heard a door open and close. I had a feeling it was the basement door.

It was a while later that I heard the door open and close again and then heavy slow footsteps coming up the creaky stairs. The footsteps once again came to my door then stopped.

I sat up once again to listen and I could hear creaks of pressure on the floor outside the door and then I heard the doorknob start to turn. I lay back down and pulled the sheets over me and pretended to be asleep.

I heard Evelyn take a few steps into the room, pause and then turn to go back out. I heard her go back to her room and shut the door.

I was a bit disturbed as this was very bizarre behavior. I waited about half an hour before deciding I had to see what was in that basement.

I got out of the rickety bed, tiptoed to the door and then tiptoed down the stairs. I opened the heavy basement door, flipped on the lights and crept down the stairs. I made it to the bottom step.

Suddenly, I had to hold in the urge to scream. There were two old wooden chairs dead center in the basement and there were two of what I could only describe as decaying corpses with wigs on them sitting in them.

The sight of a bug crawling on one of them made me want to puke. I brought myself to walk deeper into the basement closer to the corpses. I had to make sure they were real.

Both of the corpses had men's wigs on them. The bigger of the two also had a beret on. I don't know much about corpses or their rate of decaying but I'd say these corpses were both almost a year old.

I felt like my heart stopped momentarily when I heard footsteps coming from upstairs on the first floor. I couldn't make it to the light switch because I had no time so I hid behind one of the couches in the basement.

As I heard slow heavy footsteps coming down one creepy step at a time I had my hands covering my mouth to keep from screaming.

Just then I heard Evelyn whisper my name. A few seconds later she did it again all the while moving closer to my position.

I looked around the couch and saw Evelyn was already halfway across the basement with a big kitchen knife in her hand.

I knew she would be too slow to catch me so I ran for it to the stairs. She screamed my name as she tried to cut me with the knife as I ran past. She was too slow and I was running on pure adrenaline. I heard her behind me, following as fast as she could.

When I made it to the first floor of the house I ran upstairs to my bedroom to grab my backpack. By the time I ran back downstairs Evelyn was at the top basement step.

I ran out the front door and to my car. I turned it on, caught my breath, looked to the front door of the big old house and saw that crazy old lady standing there waving the knife around.

I drove off the huge property and down the road making it back home within 10 minutes. I called the police and told them everything.

Several weeks later I found out through one of the investigating officers that one of those corpses belonged to Evelyn's dead husband. The smaller corpse belonged to a young woman who went missing a year ago. She was a freelance maid.

STORY 8

IN THE WOODS

I went to Binghamton University for two years and I quickly made a big group of friends there. We'd go out every weekend to chill out and have some fun after a long week of studies.

One weekend on a Friday night in October, me and two other close friends decided to hang out in the school nature preserve by the lake. There was this little clearing on the far side of the lake that was convenient for fires since it was so far from view of the school or campus security.

Kids would sometimes, but not often come here to smoke pot, drink and do basically all the things teenagers like to do. It was a relatively unknown spot on campus by most and we liked that about it.

That night we just brought a bunch of beers, lit a fire and hung out. As the night progressed time seemed to pass quicker as the alcohol began to take effect.

Eventually it got to the point where we were all laughing so hard that one of my two friends was on the floor rolling in the leaves. That was when my other friend stopped laughing and put his finger to his lips, "Shhhhh".

We all perked up and listened. We heard the crunching of leaves and branches in the distance. We threw our bottles in the lake since we were all under 21 and it wasn't unheard of for campus police to come through the woods on weekend's to catch kids doing drugs.

We put the rest of the beers into a backpack to keep them hidden. I was moderately drunk so my paranoia was higher than usual, that was probably the case for all of us. The fire exposed us to anyone passing through the woods but the spot was so unknown and far from campus that it was rare to find anybody else that deep in the woods.

It sounded like just one person in the distance. The sound of a tree branch snapping not too far away freaked all of us out. None of us were really the confrontational ones from our group so we lacked the confidence to stand up and yell out to try to scare whoever it was away.

Instead we all just sat in silence. We heard what seemed to be somebody or something circling us or at least walking around in a c-shape around our little campsite. It literally started to feel like we were in the movie The Blair Witch Project because the sounds we heard were very similar.

There were more cracking tree branches and leaves crunching on the ground which kept echoing over to our campsite. We laughed about it at first but I personally soon became terrified of who or what it could be out there.

Suddenly, a huge thud made all three of us jump. At first I didn't understand even though I saw what caused the sound it took me a few seconds to digest the fact that a branch had been thrown into the center of our little fire site.

One of my two friends took off running while my other friend and I sat still looking at each other, half laughing and half concerned. We didn't know yet if this was some kind of joke or not.

Then my friend let out a scream of pain as he was struck in the face by another tree branch. I grabbed the backpack, helped my friend up off the ground and we hauled ass back in the direction of our dorm.

When we made it to the road separating the nature preserve from our dorm we stopped to catch our breath but whoever was out there proved to be following us because I heard running footsteps coming closer.

We continued to run back to the dorm and when we got back to our floor we found our other friend in his room already, scared out of his mind.

We looked out of his room window down towards the edge of the woods where we had just come from. There was what looked like a well-built man crouched on all fours moving back and forth.

I couldn't see too well because of the darkness but it looked like he was wearing some sort of gorilla or monkey costume. He seemed to be covered in fur.

Right at that second whoever that was looked upwards directly at us. We all ducked under the window. A few minutes later I slowly stood up to take another look. Whoever it was went back into the woods. We never went back into the woods again after that.

STORY 9

WHAT MADE THE NOISES?

My family and I are probably the biggest skeptics in the world, which is why I can't explain what happened on this particular day.

My brother and I were in our house. I went downstairs and he was in the kitchen. I grabbed a glass of water and asked him if he believed in ghosts. He shook his head but told me a story about something that he thinks may seem paranormal.

Then I looked at him and asked, "Did you ever try to scare me when I came home from school?"

"I did, once," he said.

He continued by saying, "But all I did was shoot a Nerf gun bullet at you while you were on the computer."

I wish he didn't say that because it was not what I remember happened to me.

When I was in the seventh grade I do remember him shooting a Nerf gun at me but it felt inferior to what I was about to tell him.

I continued to speak with him about the story that follows. It happened in middle school when I was in seventh grade.

I came home from school one day and went to my bedroom where I sat on my bed and put in earphones to watch YouTube videos.

My mom had called me to tell me that my brother would be gone or would be leaving soon to go to a friend's house. My parents also worked late which meant I would be home alone.

I was a very quiet kid when no one was around because I always had this fear that there could be someone in the house with me. If I didn't make much noise then they couldn't find me…right?

Anyway, I paused my YouTube video and headed to the bathroom. Before I go on, just to clarify, the house was fitted with motion detectors. An alarm would activate if any doors or windows are opened. A special electronic signal box will immediately display which door has been used.

I was in the bathroom and right about to flush the toilet when I heard a loud thud come from my brother's room. I assumed that he must be about to leave for his friend's house so I flushed the toilet and got up to wash my hands.

After a few seconds I realized that there were no more noises, the house fell still but I felt like I was being listened to or watched.

I turned off the tap and walked over to the bathroom door to lock it. Something felt wrong. My stomach started to ache from fear. I felt like I was just being paranoid but I also couldn't shake that weird feeling in my gut, so I waited for another noise.

I didn't have my phone on me so I couldn't text my brother. We had a house phone but it made loud noises when you dialed so I didn't want to risk it.

Suddenly, I heard talking coming from my brother's room; but that was not my brother talking. It couldn't have been my mom or dad because they were at work.

The muttering was deep and low and it sent shivers down my spine. Who was in my brother's room?

Then there was a slow pounding noise that started getting closer to the bathroom door. It stopped dead in its tracks right at the door. I moved myself away from the door near the window hoping that if it busted in I could escape.

I couldn't fight whoever it was since I was a weak 7th grader so that was out of the question. I covered my mouth to keep from breathing loudly in case they didn't know I was in the bathroom.

The footsteps then continued to make their way to the stairway and then stopped. I heard a loud crashing noise from what I thought was the middle platform of the stairs and then again at the bottom.

The muttering stopped and the loud footsteps made their way to the front door of the house. I heard the door open and close. The sensory alarm went off and then stopped after 5 beeps.

I didn't know if it was safe or not so I made my way to the door and rested my hands on the doorknob still covering my mouth. To the left of me towards the ground is a laundry chute that led to our laundry room, if someone were to get from the main floor to the laundry room it would definitely take over 30 seconds. However, about 10 seconds after the door opened and closed a vicious jabbing noise pounded at the small laundry chute door.

I stood there in shock, not sure what to do. It sounded like someone took the end of a broom and reached up there to stab at the door from the other side.

I watched as the pounding of the door vibrated the small laundry chute door hoping that it wouldn't bust open. Then it suddenly stopped.

I stayed in the bathroom for what seemed like an eternity and then quietly crept to my room to call my parents. No one picked up so I waited for them to get home.

I held onto my door handle to make sure no one could get in since I didn't have a lock on it. When my parents got home they didn't believe a word I said of course.

Telling this story to my brother now made his mouth drop. He continued to tell me that he used to hear things come from the attic that used to open up in his bedroom.

I will honestly never forget that day. Me and my brother can't figure out who or what that was and I try not to think too hard about it either. I still don't quite know what happened and I may never know.

STORY 10

WATCHING EYES

As a kid I lived with my mom who was a single mother. Money was a little tight as mom had to take care of four kids. I was the youngest so I had the smallest room.

My room was next to the den which was a small square room with wood flooring. There were two big vents in the floor in this room and two vents in the ceiling. My bed took up half the room.

I was 12 years old at the time, doing my homework on my bed when I heard a child's laughter. I went outside my room to look around the den and kitchen for any of my siblings; everyone seemed to be upstairs.

Usually in these kinds of stories you hear people say they just chalk these things up to their imagination, but I definitely heard that laughter. There's no way I imagined something so clear.

I continued my homework, but with one ear perked up listening for any other suspicious sounds. Eventually enough time passed that I was able to move past it and forget about the whole thing…until I heard the child's laughter again.

This time it was louder and there was even more giggling. I want to also point out that it went on for much longer too.

Then I realized that the laughter wasn't coming from outside my room, it was somewhere inside the room. I figured one of my brothers was hiding from me and playing some kind of prank.

I followed the sound of the laughter and it led me to the corner of my room. I looked down at the vent on the floor; the sound was coming from inside the vent.

I got down on my knees and pressed my ear up to the vent. There was no more giggling at this point. There was total silence for a few seconds. I lifted my ear from the vent and put my eyes up to the vent to get a peek inside.

It took me a second to realize I was staring at a pair of large yellow eyes looking back up at me. I shrieked and screamed for my mom. She came storming into my room moments later but of course the noises had stopped and those large yellow eyes in the vent had disappeared.

My mom let me sleep in her room that night. In fact, that went on for a week before she put her foot down and told me to stop being so silly.

I spent the next four years sleeping in that same bedroom before we moved. I never heard the laughter again, but I will never forget those yellow eyes looking up at me.

MORE BOOKS IN THE CREEPY STORY HOUR COLLECTION...

**Scary Short Stories for Teens
Book 1**

**Scary Short Stories for Teens
Book 3**